Identity Kit

An Anthology about Identity

Anthology

PM Anthology
Ruby

U.S. Edition © 2013 HMH Supplemental Publishers
10801 N. MoPac Expressway
Building #3
Austin, TX 78759
www.hmhsupplemental.com

Text © 2001 Cengage Learning Australia Pty Limited
Illustrations © 2001 Cengage Learning Australia Pty Limited
Originally published in Australia by Cengage Learning Australia

6 7 8 9 10   1957   16 15 14
4500487833

Text:
Design: design rescue
Photographs: Lindsay Edwards
Cover illustration: Ian Forss
Printed in China by 1010 Printing International Ltd

Acknowledgments
The publisher would like to acknowledge the following authors and publishers for their permission to reprint extracts from the titles below for this anthology:

The Midnight Fox by Betsy Byars, Puffin, England, 1976; Chinese Cinderella - The Secret Story of an Unwanted Daughter by Adeline Yen Mah, Puffin, Australia, 1999; Hatchet by Gary Paulsen, Macmillan Children's Books, London, 1987; 'Me I Am!' by Jack Prelutsky from The Walker Book of Poetry, Walker Books, London, 1983; 'Truth' by Barrie Wade from One Hundred Years of Poetry for Children, Oxford University Press, London; Charlotte's Web by E.B. White, Hamish Hamilton, 1952.

Every effort has been made to trace and acknowledge copyright, but in some cases we have been unsuccessful. The publishers apologise for any accidental infringement and welcome information to redress the situation.

Identity Kit: An Anthology about Identity
ISBN 978 0 76 357803 9

Contents

ME I AM!   4

The Attack   6

Acting Up   14

Chinese Cinderella   22

Truth   36

The Same, but Different   38

Abandoned!   48

Charlotte's Breakfast   61

ME I AM!

Jack Prelutsky

Illustrated by Margaret Power

I am the only ME I AM
who qualifies as me;
no ME I AM has been before,
and none will ever be.

No other ME I AM can feel
the feelings I've within;
no other ME I AM can fit
precisely in my skin.

There is no other ME I AM
who thinks the thoughts I do;
the world contains one ME I AM,
there is no room for two.

I am the only ME I AM
this earth shall ever see;
that ME I AM I always am
is no one else but ME!

The Attack

Gary Paulsen   Illustrated by Mini Goss

Brian is the only survivor of a terrifying small plane crash. Now he's alone in the wilderness, with only a hatchet to help him survive. Brian is a city kid, and he isn't used to roughing it. At first, he's not sure he can survive, but his will to live is strong. Hatchet *is Brian's story of determination and courage.*

Setting the Scene

It's the middle of night, and the wind is blowing through the pine trees. Brian is sleeping in a makeshift shelter that he constructed—it's the only place he felt safe, until now. Something has entered his shelter...

At first Brian thought it was a growl. In the still darkness of the shelter in the middle of the night his eyes came open and he was awake and he thought there was a growl. But it was the wind, a medium wind in the pines had made some sound that brought him up, brought him awake. He sat up and was hit with the smell.

It terrified him. The smell was one of rot, some musty rot that made him think only of graves with cobwebs and dust and old death. His nostrils widened and he opened his eyes wider but he could see nothing. It was too dark, too hard dark with clouds covering even the small light from the stars, and he could not see. But the smell was alive, alive and full and in the shelter. He thought of the bear, thought of Bigfoot and every monster he had ever seen in every horror movie he had ever watched, and his heart hammered in his throat.

7

Then he heard the slithering. A brushing sound, a slithering brushing sound near his feet—and he kicked out as hard as he could, kicked out and threw the hatchet at the sound, a noise coming from his throat. But the hatchet missed, sailed into the wall where it hit the rocks with a shower of sparks, and his leg was instantly torn with pain, as if a hundred needles had been driven into it. "Unnnngh!"

Now he screamed, with the pain and fear, and skittered on his backside up into the corner of the shelter, breathing through his mouth, straining to see, to hear.

The slithering moved again, he thought toward him at first, and terror took him, stopping his breath. He felt he could see a low dark form, a bulk in the darkness, a shadow that lived, but now it moved away, slithering and scraping it moved away and he saw or thought he saw it go out of the door opening.

He lay on his side for a moment, then pulled a rasping breath in and held it, listening for the attacker to return. When it was apparent that the shadow wasn't coming back he felt the calf of his leg, where the pain was centered and spreading to fill the whole leg.

His fingers gingerly touched a group of needles that had been driven through his pants and into the fleshy part of his calf. They were stiff and very sharp on the ends that stuck out, and he knew then what the attacker had been. A porcupine had stumbled into his shelter and when he had kicked it the thing had slapped him with its tail of quills.

He touched each quill carefully. The pain made it seem as if dozens of them had been slammed into his leg, but there were only eight, pinning the cloth against his skin. He leaned back against the wall for a minute. He couldn't leave them in, they had to come out, but just touching them made the pain more intense.

So fast, he thought. So fast things change. When he'd gone to sleep he had satisfaction and in just a moment it was all different. He grasped one of the quills, held his breath, and jerked. It sent pain signals to his brain in tight waves, but he grabbed another, pulled it, then another quill. When he had pulled four of them he stopped for a moment. The pain had gone from being a pointed injury pain to spreading in a hot smear up his leg and it made him catch his breath.

Some of the quills were driven in deeper than others and they tore when they came out. He breathed deeply twice, let half of the breath out, and went back to work. Jerk, pause, jerk—and three more times before he lay back in the darkness, done. The pain filled his leg now, and with it came new waves of self-pity. Sitting alone in the dark, his leg aching, some mosquitoes finding him again, he started crying. It was all too much, just too much, and he couldn't take it. Not the way it was.

I can't take it this way, alone with no fire and in the dark, and next time it might be something worse, maybe a bear, and it wouldn't be just quills in the leg, it would be worse. I can't do this, he thought, again and again. I can't. Brian pulled himself up until he was sitting upright back in the corner of the cave. He put his head down on his arms across his knees, with stiffness taking his left leg, and cried until he was cried out.

He did not know how long it took, but later he looked back on this time of crying in the corner of the dark cave and thought of it as when he learned the most important rule of survival, which was that feeling sorry for yourself didn't work. It wasn't that it was wrong to do, or that it was considered incorrect. It was more than that—it didn't work. When he sat alone in the darkness and cried and was done, was all done with it, nothing had changed. His leg still hurt, it was still dark, he was still alone and the self-pity had accomplished nothing.

(Excerpt taken from *Hatchet* by Gary Paulsen, Macmillan Children's Books, London, England, 1987)

Acting Up

Sally Morrell   Photographs by Lindsay Edwards

HOW DO YOU BECOME ANOTHER PERSON—ESPECIALLY WHEN YOU ARE STILL LEARNING ABOUT THE PERSON YOU ARE?

Eleven-year-old Nathan Derrick does it all the time. As a professional actor, he has to become someone else every time he takes on a new job.

Nathan has played many different roles—from a polite, well-behaved Austrian schoolboy in the musical *The Sound of Music* to a filthy young thief in the musical *Les Miserables*.

"It's not really that hard to be someone else," Nathan says.

But, he admits, it takes a bit of homework to make a character look believable to the audience.

"You don't just go on stage and become that person without having to think about who that person is," he says. "You have to work out who they are and try to understand them so you can then be them as an actor."

Nathan says he was taught the "Who, What, Where, When, Why and How" approach to acting by one of his directors and it has always worked with him.

"First, I sit down and think about who the character is and what they are doing in the musical or the play," he says. "Then I think about the setting of the musical or play. *The Sound of Music* was set in Austria in 1938, so I learned about that time. Then I thought about why my character says things, and how and why my character acts the way he does."

Nathan discusses the "Who, What, Where, When, Why and How" approach to acting.

"I was playing Kurt, one of the children, so we talked about how all the children were pretty well-behaved and stuff. It helped us all get into character," Nathan says.

As part of their on-the-job schooling by a tutor, the children also did a project on their character.

"That helped as well. I had to give my character a real-life history, as if I was telling his story," Nathan says.

"I had to think about when Kurt would have been born and what his life would have been like. It was good because it helped Kurt become real."

Everyone in the musical was called by his or her character's name during the six-week rehearsal time and for the length of the musical's run.

"Other people in the cast called me Kurt. I called my friend Emily, Brigitta, and my friend, Maddy, Gretel. That way we could feel like a family and relate to each other like brothers and sisters," he says.

But Nathan says he didn't feel that Kurt, his character, was taking over too much of his life.

"Oh, no, once I got in the car to go home I was back to being Nathan again. Kurt didn't take over, it was just a way for all of us to get into our characters," he says.

Nathan and his poster from *The Sound of Music* signed by the other cast and crew members.

Nathan (middle row, second from left) and other cast members from *The Sound of Music*.

Nathan continued going to school during the run of performances but often left mid-morning for a matinee, or after lunch so he could sleep before that night's performance.

"But I didn't mind not being around school that much," he says.

And that's not because he finds the work hard—even with the missed hours, he tries to keep up with all his schoolwork. It's just that his classmates haven't been very supportive of his chosen career.

"I don't have many friends at school. My best friend, Eammon, is also an actor, but he goes to another school," he says. "The kids at my school ignore it all, but I'm used to it by now."

Even when Nathan made the front page of the city newspaper, no one at school mentioned it, not even the teachers.

"I think Mom and Dad get more upset than I do. They get hurt for me, but I don't let it bother me that much," he says. "But I think if I was on the front page because I could run fast or was good at football, it wouldn't be like this."

Calling all yodellers

All in the (Von Trapp) family: brothers Nathan, 10, and Brodie, 8, and sisters Saasha, 10, and Tarah, 9, practise for Sunday's auditions at Her Majesty's and, below, the original *Sound of Music* cast. Picture: CRAIG BORROW

ARE you a courageous, fearless youngster whose favorite things include dancing and singing?

If so, you may find yourself playing alongside Lisa McCune in the $6 million Melbourne production of *The Sound of Music* next March.

All dressed up and ready to go yesterday were brothers Nathan and Brodie and sisters Saasha and Tarah, who confessed to watching the film "about a million times".

Auditions start at Her Majesty's in Exhibition St at 11.30am on Sunday for the roles of the six younger Von Trapps — Friedrich, Louisa, Kurt, Brigitta, Marta and Gretl — aged 6-14.

Nathan wants to continue acting and singing when he leaves school.

"My younger brother, Brodie, started acting and I sort of followed him into it. I found I really liked it," he says.

His first big production was playing the young Peter Allen in *The Boy from Oz*. Nathan was nine-years-old at the time.

"I learned a lot from that. At first I wasn't sure how you went about being someone else, but I watched a whole lot of videos of Peter Allen and tried to learn about him," he says.

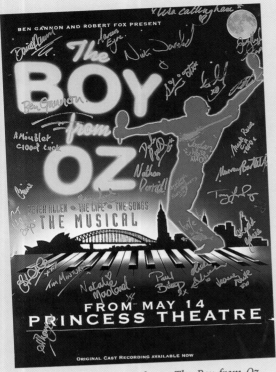
Nathan's signed poster from *The Boy from Oz*.

"The director told me the most important thing was to enjoy myself and to have fun, and that was great," he says.

Nathan really enjoyed himself. So much so that, when *The Boy from Oz* ended, he felt desperately unhappy.

"It was *really* hard. I missed the friends I had made, I missed the music, and I missed being the character," he says.

Nathan became so depressed that his parents worried about him. But before long, *The Sound of Music* came up and kept him busy for almost half a year.

"When that finished it was also really hard, but this time I was more ready for it," he says.

To keep busy, Nathan took a role in an amateur production of the French musical *Les Miserables*. He played the dirty little thief, Gavroche, who lives alone on the streets of Paris in the years leading up to the French Revolution.

"It's quite a change from Kurt, but that's good. This time I'm a really bad character!" he says.

Nathan says the most important thing about being an actor is to enjoy what you are doing. It's also important not to get too caught up in "acting" as your character.

"Basically, you should have fun and be yourself. You have to act as your character, but you have to make it believable. You have to be natural," he says.

"If you've done all the work before-hand, thinking about who you are as the character, then you shouldn't have to act—you should just be natural."

Nathan bought Ozzie, his golden retriever, with his earnings from *The Boy from Oz*.

Chinese Cinderella

Adeline Yen Mah   Illustrated by Xiangyi Mo

Adeline Yen Mah's mother died while giving birth to her. From that moment, Adeline's family considered her bad luck. Chinese Cinderella *is an autobiographical story of Adeline's struggle to prove her worth and value to a family that barely acknowledges her at all.*

Setting the Scene

It's 1941, and the young Adeline (Wu Mei) lives with her family in Tianjin, a city port on the northern coast of China. She has just started school and has been awarded a medal for being at the top of her class.

Characters

Ye Ye

Nai Nai

Father

Niang

Aunt Baba

Big Brother

Second Brother

Third Brother

Fourth Brother

Big Sister

Adeline
(Wu Mei)

Little Sister

As soon as I got home from school, Aunt Baba noticed the silver medal dangling from the left pocket of my uniform. She was combing her hair in front of the mirror in our room when I rushed in and plopped my school bag on my bed.

"What's that hanging on your dress?"

"It's something that Mother Agnes gave me in front of the whole class this afternoon. She called it an award."

My aunt looked thrilled. "So soon? You only started kindergarten one week ago. What it is for?"

"It's for being at the top of my class for this week. When Mother Agnes pinned it on my dress, she said I could wear it for seven days. Here, this certificate goes with it." I opened my school bag and handed her an envelope as I climbed onto her lap.

She opened the envelope and took out the certificate.

"Why, it's all written in French or English or some other foreign language. How do you expect me to read this, my precious little treasure?" I knew she was pleased because she was smiling as she hugged me. "One day soon," she continued, "you'll be able to translate all this into Chinese for me. Until then, we'll just write today's date on the envelope and put it away somewhere safe. Go close the door properly and put on the latch so no one will come in."

I watched her open her closet door and take out her safe-deposit box. She took the key from a gold chain around her neck and placed my certificate underneath her jade bracelet, pearl necklace, and diamond watch—as if my award were also some precious jewel impossible to replace.

The dinner bell rang at seven. Aunt Baba took my hand and led me into the dining room.

I went to the foot of the table and sat at my assigned seat between Second Brother and Third Brother as my three brothers ran in, laughing and jostling each other. I cringed as Second Brother sat down on my right. He was always saying mean things to me and grabbing my share of goodies when nobody was looking.

26

Second Brother used to sit next to Big Brother but the two of them fought a lot. Father finally separated them when they broke a fruit bowl fighting over a pear.

Big Brother winked at me as he sat down. He had a twinkle in his eye and was whistling a tune. Yesterday he'd tried to teach me how to whistle but no matter how hard I tried I couldn't make it work. Was Big Brother up to some new mischief today?

Third Brother took his seat on my left. His lips were pursed and he was trying to whistle unsuccessfully. Seeing the medal on my uniform, he raised his eyebrow and smiled at me. "What's that?" he asked.

"It's an award for being the top of my class. My teacher says I can wear it for seven days."

"Congratulations! First week at school and you get a medal! Not bad!"

While I was basking in Third Brother's praise, I suddenly felt a hard blow across the back of my head. I turned around to see Second Brother glowering at me.

"What did you do *that* for?" I asked angrily.

Deliberately, he took my right arm under the table and gave it a quick, hard twist while no one was looking. "Because I feel like it, that's why, you ugly little squirt! This'll teach you to show off your medal!"

I turned for help from Third Brother but he was looking straight ahead, obviously not wishing to be involved. At that moment, Father, Niang, and Big Sister came in together and Second Brother immediately let go of my arm.

Niang was speaking to Big Sister in English and Big Sister was nodding assent. She glanced at all of us smugly as she took her seat between Second Brother and Niang, full of her own self-importance at being so favored by our stepmother. Because her left arm had been paralyzed from a birth injury, her movements were slow and awkward and she liked to order me, or Third Brother, to carry out her chores.

"Wu Mei (Fifth Younger Sister)!" she now said. "Go fetch my English–Chinese dictionary. It's on my bed in my room. Niang wants me to translate something…"

I was halfway off my chair when Nai Nai said, "Do the translation later! Sit down, Wu Mei. Let's have dinner first before the food gets cold. Here, let me first pick a selection of soft foods to send up to the nursery so the nurse can feed the two youngest …" She turned to Niang with a smile. "Another two years and all seven grandchildren will be sitting around this table. Won't that be wonderful?"

Niang's two-year-old son, Fourth Brother, and her infant daughter, Little Sister, were still too young to eat with us. However, they were already "special" from the moment of their birth. Though nobody actually said so, it was simply understood that everyone considered Niang's "real" children to be better-looking, smarter, and simply superior in every way to Niang's stepchildren. Besides, who dared disagree?

For dessert, the maids brought in a huge bowl of my favorite fruit, dragons' eyes! I was so happy I couldn't help laughing out loud.

Nai Nai gave us each a small bowl of fruit and I counted seven dragons' eyes in mine. I peeled off the leathery brown skin and was savoring the delicate white flesh when Father suddenly pointed to my medal.

"Is this medal for being at the top of your class?" he asked.

I nodded eagerly, too excited to speak. A hush fell upon the table. This was the first time anyone could remember Father singling me out or saying anything to me. Everyone looked at my medal.

"Is the left side of your chest heavier?" Father continued, beaming with pride. "Are you tilting?"

I flushed with pleasure and could barely swallow. My big Dia Dia was actually teasing me! On his way out, he even patted me on my head. Then he said, "Continue studying hard and bringing honor to our Yen family name so we can be proud of you."

All the grown-ups beamed at me as they followed Father out of the room. How wonderful! I must study harder and keep wearing this medal so I can go on pleasing Father, I thought to myself.

But what was this? Big Sister was coming toward me with a scowl. Without a word, she reached over and snatched two dragons' eyes from my bowl as she left the room. My three brothers followed her example. Then they all ran out, leaving me quite alone with my silver medal, staring at my empty bowl.

(Excerpt from *Chinese Cinderella – The Secret Story of an Unwanted Daughter* by Adeline Yen Mah, Puffin, Australia, 1999)

Adeline (Wu Mei) finished her schooling in England. She studied medicine in London and immigrated to the United States where she practiced as a physician for twenty-six years. She is now an internationally successful writer.

Truth

Barrie Wade   Illustrated by Anna Wilson

Sticks and stones may break my bones,
but words can also hurt me.
Stones and sticks break only skin,
while words are ghosts that haunt me.

Slant and curved the word-swords fall
to pierce and stick inside me.
Bats and bricks may ache through bones,
but words can mortify me.

Pain from words has left its scar
on mind and heart that's tender.
Cuts and bruises now have healed;
it's words that I remember.

You're wrong

You're stupid

I don't like you

You're weird

Go away!

You'll never amount to anything

The Same, but Different

Sally Morrell

Photographs by Lindsay Edwards

Identical twins Ashleigh and Caitlin Roberts have very different views about what it's like to look exactly the same as someone else.

"I really like looking like Ashleigh. I just like being like her," says Caitlin.

But Ashleigh doesn't like being a twin. "I don't like looking the same as someone else all the time. I'd much rather look different," she says. "People say all the time, 'Oh, I'd love to be a twin,' but I don't like it. I'd want to have Cait as my sister, but I'd rather not be a twin."

> "I really like looking like Ashleigh.
> I just like being like her."

Caitlin says she feels special being a twin. "It's not just looking the same that I like, it's also having someone to play with when you get home and when you go away. I just really love being a twin," she says.

> "I'd much rather look different...
> I'd want to have Cait as my sister,
> but I'd rather not be a twin."

Caitlin doesn't mind that Ashleigh doesn't like being a twin as much as she does. "It doesn't bother me, really. She's always felt that way," she says.

The 10-year-old twins are indeed a mirror image of each other. They both have long brown hair, the same brown eyes, and the same wide smile. The only difference is the pattern of freckles that dots their noses. But you would have to be right up close to them to be able to figure out who was who.

Ashleigh says that even in their own family, not everyone can tell them apart.

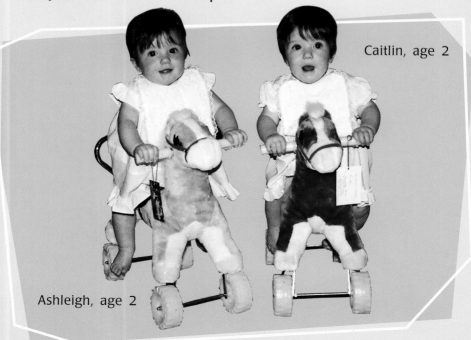

Caitlin, age 2

Ashleigh, age 2

Even in their own family, not everyone can tell them apart.

"Mom always can. I don't know how she does it but she does, even when we have our backs turned. Dad still can't tell us apart most of the time," Ashleigh says. "Sometimes he gets it right, but usually he can't tell the difference. It doesn't matter to me."

But it matters to Caitlin. "You can tell sometimes he's just guessing. I guess I'm used to it, but it does still bother me a bit. I get a bit annoyed," she says.

Their eight-year-old brother, Christopher, gets it right almost all the time, but the twins say their dog, Kelsey, is never wrong.

When Caitlin and Ashleigh started school, they both had to wear the same uniform. Teachers and students couldn't tell them apart.

"Everyone kept getting us mixed up all the time. I didn't like it," says Ashleigh.

After two years of being in the same class, the girls wanted a change. They asked to be separated, at least for one year to give it a try.

"It's great," says Ashleigh. "I don't want to be in the same class again."

Caitlin says that while it was annoying that the other children and the teachers mixed them up, she really didn't mind that much. She would even be happy to share a class with her sister again.

"But we won't be in the same class again," Ashleigh insists. "Mom promised."

Caitlin has lots of friends at school.

Before they went into different classes, the girls preferred to play with each other. But once they went their separate ways, they started making new friends.

Ashleigh became especially close to one friend, Bree, a new girl at the school.

"When Bree arrived at the school, I had to show her around, and she liked playing with me and I liked playing with her. Since then we've been best friends," Ashleigh says.

While Caitlin has lots of friends at school, she has no special friend. "Ash is my best friend," she says.

Ashleigh knows that Caitlin and Bree aren't good friends, but she says it doesn't worry her. "Bree says Caitlin is different than me. I can't help that," she says.

Ashleigh became especially close to one friend.

43

Caitlin admits it makes her sad that she is no longer her sister's best friend. "I'm disappointed it happened," she says. "But I've talked about it with Mom. Anyway, there's not much I can do about it."

But Caitlin has made many other new friends who are not in the same group as Bree and Ashleigh.

"It's nice because they can tell us apart. It's easier because they always know who I am."

You would think that because the girls look exactly the same they would have similar personalities, but they don't. Caitlin is the more reserved of the twins, but she is also the most determined.

Caitlin is the most determined.

Ashleigh is very outgoing and it doesn't seem like she would ever be bothered by much. Caitlin is quieter and is very particular about what she likes and doesn't like. She is more concerned about appearance, while Ashleigh is just starting to get interested in hairstyles and clothes.

The twins also never dress the same, even by accident.

"We go separately when we go with Mom to buy clothes. That way we won't buy the same things or, I guess, want to buy the same things," says Ashleigh. "But we always come back with different things anyway. I guess we have different tastes."

Ashleigh is very outgoing.

Caitlin was the bigger baby and for a long time was slightly bigger than her sister. Now, Ashleigh is one size bigger in shoes and a half inch taller than her sister.

Even though Ashleigh would rather not have been born a twin, she says it does have its advantages.

QUICK QUESTIONS

Name: Caitlin Roberts

What is your favorite color?

Lime Green

What is your favorite food?

Peppers

Do you have a hero? Who is she/he and why?

Cathy Freeman (Olympic runner)—I like to run!

What is your favorite music group/singer?

Anastasia

What is your favorite animal?

Dog

"Well, there's always someone to play with. When you get home from school, when you go away for holidays, you always have someone there to play with. Last time we went to the beach, we could boogie-board together. I like that," she says.

"I love it," says Caitlin.

QUICK QUESTIONS

Name: Ashleigh Roberts

What is your favorite color?
Yellow

What is your favorite food?
Bananas

Do you have a hero? Who is she/he and why?
Cathy Freeman—I want to be a runner when I grow up.

What is your favorite music group/singer?
Five

What is your favorite animal?
Dog

Abandoned!

Betsy Byars   Illustrated by Chantal Stewart

Tom's parents are going to Europe, so Tom has to spend the summer at his aunt and uncle's farm. Tom is a sensitive boy whose father criticizes him for not being tough and in control of his emotions. Tom has one good friend, Petie, back home, but now he won't even have Petie to help him through the summer.

Setting the Scene

Tom's parents have just brought him to the farm and are preparing to leave. He feels lonely and abandoned. He's worried he might cry, but he has to be brave...

"You're not leaving!" Aunt Millie said. My feelings exactly.

"We have to."

"But we wanted you at least to stay the night."

"We can't. That's what we wanted to do," Mom said, "but the couple we're riding to New York with wants to leave first thing in the morning. Tom says he doesn't mind, but I feel awful just dropping him and running."

"Oh, now, Tom is going to get along fine, aren't you, Tom?"

"Sure."

49

Identity Kit

We walked out on the porch without saying anything, but at the steps Mom said, "Now you be a real good boy, Tom, and do what Aunt Millie tells you."

"I will."

"We'll get on just fine," Aunt Millie said, patting my shoulder again.

"I know." Mom hugged Aunt Millie and said, "This is the nicest thing that anyone has ever done for me." Then she hugged me real hard, got into the car, and turned her face away.

My dad said, "Well, so long, sport," and socked me on the arm.

I said, "Have a nice trip." I was pleased that my nose wasn't running or anything, because I felt terrible.

My dad started the car and they drove off. Mom kept her head turned, but Dad waved and honked the horn all the way to the highway.

Aunt Millie went back into the house and I sat on the steps. My dad was always talking about control. He said control was the most important thing there was to an athlete, and he was always telling me I should have more of it. I couldn't imagine anyone having more control than it took to sit quietly on the steps, nose and eyes dry, while being abandoned.

Sometimes my dad would get real disgusted with me because I didn't control myself too well. I used to cry pretty easily if I got hurt or if something was worrying me.

I remembered one time when Petie Burkis came over to my house and told me that he knew a way that you could figure out when you were going to die—the very day! He learned this from a sitter he'd had the night before. It was all according to the wrinkles in your hand—you counted them a certain way. Well, we sat right down and counted the wrinkles in my hand. It took over an hour, and it came out that I was going to die in my seventy-ninth year, on either the eighty-second or eighty-third day. Petie said probably I would fall terribly ill on the eighty-second and last just after midnight on the eighty-third.

Then we started counting the wrinkles in Petie's hand. He had a peculiar hand, and it came out that he was going to die on the two hundred and seventy-ninth day of his ninth year. Well, Petie was nine years old right then, so he said, "Get a calendar, quick, get a calendar," and he looked like he was already getting sick.

We looked all over the house before we finally found a wallet-sized insurance calendar, and then we got down on our stomachs and began to count the days. We were saying the numbers together—two hundred and seventy-six, two hundred and seventy-seven, two hundred and seventy-eight—and I can still hear the terrible way it sounded when we both said, "two hundred and seventy-nine." It was like the last sound in the world, because it turned out that Petie was going to die on the next Saturday.

I said, "Let's do it again."

We did it again, very slowly and carefully this time, but it still came out the same—two hundred and seventy-nine, next Saturday.

Petie felt awful, I could see that, and I felt even worse, and if there had been any way in the world I could give him nineteen or twenty of my seventy-nine years, I would have done it in a minute. He said, "I better get home," like he meant, "before something happens," and then he left and I was too upset to try and stop him. I went into the house and my mom said, "What's wrong now?"

I said what was wrong was that Petie was going to die on Saturday, and right away she started laughing. I said, "Well, I certainly wouldn't think it was so hilarious if *your* best friend was going to die this Saturday," and I left the room. She caught up with me in the hall and hugged me, and then she sat down on the hall chair and made me look at her, and said, "Tommy, Petie is *not* going to die this Saturday."

"How do you know?"

"I just *know*, Tom."

"How?"

"Well, look at him. He is in perfect health. He is absolutely the healthiest boy I know."

"Healthy people are hit by cars every day, or fall down wells. You don't have to be sick to die."

"This is some fool thing you and Petie have cooked up. I think you enjoy getting all worked up about nothing."

"We do not."

"Well, I can tell you absolutely, positively that Petie is not going to die on Saturday."

"All right, then, can he come over and spend the day and night with me?" My mom was very particular about people not getting hurt in our yard. Like she would say, "I hope those little kids are not going to get hurt riding their bikes in our driveway," as if it would be perfectly all right if they were hurt just out of our drive, in the street somewhere.

"Yes, you may have him over."

This made me feel a little better, but as soon as my dad got home, he came in and talked to me for over an hour about self-control and not letting myself get worked up about foolish things. He seemed to think I enjoyed getting worked up and upset over my friend's death. I didn't want to worry about things. I wanted to be peaceful and calm like everyone else, only sometimes I couldn't.

Anyway, Petie came over on Saturday and we were careful all day. We didn't even go to bed until it was twelve o'clock. Then, before we got in bed, we went out into the hall, and in the dark we found the telephone and dialed the time to make sure. When the operator said, "The time is twelve-o-two," Petie started jumping up and down and saying, "I'm spared, I'm spared."

My dad said, "Be quiet out there."

We went in and lay down on the bed, and for about an hour all we said were things like, "Whew!" and "What a relief!" and "I really, honestly thought I was going to die, Tom, didn't you?"

I thought about that, and how now that I was controling myself perfectly, now that there could not be one single complaint of any kind about my absolutely perfect control, there was no one around to see it.

(Excerpt taken from *The Midnight Fox* by Betsy Byars, Puffin, England, 1976)

Charlotte's Breakfast

E.B. White   Illustrated by Rob Mancini

"Watch me wrap up this fly."

A fly that had been crawling along Wilbur's trough had flown up and blundered into the lower part of Charlotte's web and was tangled in the sticky threads. The fly was beating its wings furiously trying to break loose and free itself.

"First," said Charlotte, "I dive at him." She plunged headfirst toward the fly. As she dropped, a tiny silken thread unwound from her rear end.

"Next, I wrap him up." She grabbed the fly, threw a few jets of silk around it, and rolled it over and over, wrapping it so that it couldn't move. Wilbur watched in horror. He could hardly believe what he was seeing, and although he detested flies, he was sorry for this one.

"There!" said Charlotte. "Now I knock him out, so he'll be more comfortable." She bit the fly. "He can't feel a thing now," she remarked. "He'll make a perfect breakfast for me."

"You mean you *eat* flies?" gasped Wilbur.

"Certainly. Flies, bugs, grasshoppers, choice beetles, moths, butterflies, tasty cockroaches, gnats, midgets, daddy-long-legs, centipedes, mosquitoes, crickets—anything that is careless enough to get caught in my web. I have to live, don't I?"

"Why, yes, of course," said Wilbur. "Do they taste good?"

"Delicious. Of course, I don't really eat them. I drink them—drink their blood. I love blood," said Charlotte, and her pleasant, thin voice grew even thinner and more pleasant.

"Don't say that!" groaned Wilbur. "Please don't say things like that!"

"Why not? It's true, and I have to say what is true. I am not entirely happy about my diet of flies and bugs, but it's the way I'm made. A spider has to pick up a living somehow or other, and I happen to be a trapper. I just naturally build a web and trap flies and other insects. My mother was a trapper before me. Her mother was a trapper before her. All our family have been trappers. Way back for thousands and thousands of years we spiders have been laying for flies and bugs."

"It's a miserable inheritance," said Wilbur, gloomily. He was sad because his new friend was so bloodthirsty.

(Excerpt taken from *Charlotte's Web* by E. B. White, Hamish Hamilton, London, 1952)